Samuel French Acting Ed

MW00465449

Tiny Beautiful Things

Based on the Book by
Cheryl Strayed

Adapted for the Stage by
Nia Vardalos

Co-Conceived by Marshall Heyman, Thomas Kail, and Nia Vardalos

ISBN 978-0-573-70680-6

www.concordtheatricals.com
www.concordtheatricals.co.uk

be invented, including mechanical, electronic, photocopying, recording, videotaping, or otherwise, without the prior written permission of the publisher. No one shall upload this title(s), or part of this title(s), to any social media websites.

For all enquiries regarding motion picture, television, and other media rights, please contact Concord Theatricals Corp.

MUSIC USE NOTE

Licensees are solely responsible for obtaining formal written permission from copyright owners to use copyrighted music in the performance of this play and are strongly cautioned to do so. If no such permission is obtained by the licensee, then the licensee must use only original music that the licensee owns and controls. Licensees are solely responsible and liable for all music clearances and shall indemnify the copyright owners of the play(s) and their licensing agent, Concord Theatricals Corp., against any costs, expenses, losses and liabilities arising from the use of music by licensees. Please contact the appropriate music licensing authority in your territory for the rights to any incidental music.

IMPORTANT BILLING AND CREDIT REQUIREMENTS

If you have obtained performance rights to this title, please refer to your licensing agreement for important billing and credit requirements.

Original New York production by The Public Theater in New York City. Oskar Eustis, Artistic Director. Patrick Willingham, Executive Director.

TINY BEAUTIFUL THINGS premiered on November 15, 2016 in the Shiva at The Public Theater in New York City. The production was directed by Thomas Kail, with scenic design by Rachel Hauck, costume design by Jennifer Moeller, lighting design by Jeff Croiter, and sound design by Jill BC Du Boff. The production stage manager was Diane DiVita. The cast was as follows:

SUGAR . . . . Nia Vardalos
LETTER WRITERS . . . . Phillip James Brannon, Alfredo Narciso, Natalie Woolams-Torres

TINY BEAUTIFUL THINGS transferred to the Newman at The Public Theater and opened on September 19, 2017. The cast was as follows:

SUGAR . . . . Nia Vardalos
LETTER WRITERS . . . . Teddy Cañez, Hubert Point-Du Jour, Natalie Woolams-Torres

CHARACTERS

SUGAR – Female, forties.
LETTER WRITER #1 – Male, forties.
LETTER WRITER #2 – Female, twenties.
LETTER WRITER #3 – Male, twenties.

Casting is open to all genders, ethnicities, and ages.

SETTING

The play takes place over the course of one night on the bottom floor of a worn and not luxurious two-story home. There are dirty dishes in the sink, the floor is strewn with toys and food, and well-known works of literature plus used writing journals line several bookshelves.

TIME

Late evening into early morning.

COSTUMES

Sugar wears casual, comfortable clothes suitable for home. The Letter Writers also wear casual clothes, and there aren't costume changes to delineate between the different characters they play.

PLAYWRIGHT'S NOTE

While she was awaiting publication of her memoir *Wild*, the writer Cheryl Strayed sent an admiring letter to an online anonymous advice column called *Dear Sugar*. The advice columnist emailed Ms. Strayed, revealed his identity as Steve Almond, and reminded her they'd met at a writers' conference. He praised her writing, then asked if she would take over the column.

Since it was anonymous, there wouldn't be credit, and as is the case with most art, there wasn't a paycheck, yet Ms. Strayed decided to take on the challenges of writing an advice column. She changed the tone and content by combining genuine transparency and empathy. Inserting personal stories within her responses, she gave advice which was illuminating rather than instructional.

Within months, the column became enormously popular and widely admired as a compassionate and open forum was formed by this online community. Although Sugar's identity remained a mystery, writing anonymously was not a motivating factor for Ms. Strayed. Instead, her goal was to engender unadulterated advice, unencumbered by the readers' preconceptions of who she might be.

The letters were later collected in a book titled *Tiny Beautiful Things*, published after *Wild*, and both became beloved bestsellers.

The text of this play is created from the epistolary exchange of the *Dear Sugar* advice column. To arc the play and add narrative, letters have been edited, others have been combined, and new material has been written. Although Cheryl Strayed wrote the column over the span of two years, the play takes place in one night.

A few thoughts about the initial production:

Setting Sugar in her home illustrated she was a regular person navigating the complexities and challenges of life – like the people writing to her – rather than an oracle with all the correct answers. After Sugar accepted the job, the Letter Writers entered her home, as if they visited to reveal some of their deepest truths and secrets. Sugar offered counseling deep into the night, resulting in a catharsis for both her and the Letter Writers.

Sugar entered and exited via the stairs. The set of her home did not have joined walls, so rather than walk in in a conventional manner, for example, through a door, the Letter Writers entered via the spaces between the walls. When the Letter Writers weren't conversing with Sugar they did not exit, but rather sat or stood in dimly-lit areas onstage, actively listening to the discussion. The Letter Writers and Sugar performed conversationally, as if they were speaking to each other rather than writing or reading a letter. Although the text appears to be in letter format, the intention is not to suggest a pause after the greeting or before the sign-off.

At first, Sugar did not make eye contact with the Letter Writers, but rather, read along from her computer screen. Then, in the letter titled "Confused," upon hearing the word "love," Sugar made eye contact with Letter Writer #3 and later, with Letter Writer #2 when she appeared as Sugar's mother. From "Epistles 1A" and onward, Sugar saw all the Letter Writers and addressed them directly. During "Stuck," as Sugar began to settle into her role and understand that her responses were public, she often addressed the audience as well. The computer was closed halfway by Sugar while Letter Writer #3 was speaking in "Confused." Sugar did not read, type, or refer to the computer again until the final piece, "Tiny Beautiful Things."

It was decided in our production that the actors could see each other but would not touch. They congregated and moved to various areas around stage – leaning on the kitchen table, sitting on the coffee table and stairs, standing in the kitchen. The Letter Writers interacted within the space as if they were in their own homes, not Sugar's. They ate snacks, poured drinks from the refrigerator, and picked up various objects. Symbolizing the bond formed by the exchange of grief and pursuit of healing, there was one touch at the end of "Obliterated Place" which took place in the abstract and transcended the pattern.

While many of the letters are heartbreaking, there were many humorous moments directed as well, devised to provide the relief of laughter. Many of the lighter lines in the "Epistles" and letters such as "Sexy Santa" were directed as humorous to provide an ebb and flow to the play.

Our production featured an ethnically diverse and inclusive cast who played a multitude of roles. For future productions, I request that best efforts be made to include actors of all genders and all ethnicities, without age limits.

I look forward to upcoming productions in which you will interpret this play with your love, creativity, and ingenuity.

Above all, I hope you will always remember that the letters are real.

– Nia Vardalos

ACKNOWLEDGEMENTS

The book *Tiny Beautiful Things: Advice on Love and Life from Dear Sugar* by Cheryl Strayed was given to me by my friend Thomas Kail. The book had been given to Thomas by his friend Marshall Heyman.

They felt it had the potential to be a play, so together the three of us co-conceived the notion of bringing it to the stage. To turn an online column into a play, ironically, we made contact with Cheryl Strayed on social media. We met for a cup of tea and made an agreement.

I thank Cheryl, Thomas, and Marshall for entrusting me with the text and for the patience they extended to me as I continually made changes over the course of three years of workshops and performances. The resulting friendship between the four of us is the outcome for which I wished from this creative endeavor.

I admire and thank our beautiful actors and crews for their kindness, talent, and love. I have everlasting gratitude to Johanna Pfaelzer of New York Stage and Film for the workshop readings, and Oskar Eustis and all at The Public Theater for giving us a home for two consecutive seasons. I am sending heartfelt appreciation to Cheryl Strayed for her bold and audacious writing and for her candor and generosity during our rehearsal process. Thank you to Marshall for his keen eye. I'd like to especially thank Tommy Kail for his exquisite direction, friendship, and expertise in bringing this play to the New York stage.

(It is late in the evening, the house is quiet. **SUGAR** *comes down the stairs, holding two books. She has just put her children to bed and is tired. She passes a basket of laundry on the couch, turns off a lamp, gathers dirty plates and cups, takes them to the kitchen. While doing dishes, she checks email.)*

(Ding of an incoming email.)

*(***LETTER WRITER #1*** *enters.* **SUGAR** *does not see him as she reads his email.)*

LETTER WRITER #1. Hi, it's been a while since we met at that writers' conference; I hope you're doing well and writing. For the last year I have been hiding behind a computer screen anonymously giving out advice in the online column called "Dear Sugar." I know you read the column because it's received exactly one fan letter: yours. To be honest, I don't have a passion for the gig and as you know I admire your work, so I'm brazenly emailing you with a job offer: do you want to take over the column, I mean, do you want to be Sugar? As you know it's anonymous, so there's no credit and the bonus is, there's no pay. So, you in?

*(***LETTER WRITER #1*** *takes out a cell phone to check email and looks at it, waiting for a response.)*

*(***SUGAR*** *types the first line of her response as she says it.)*

SUGAR. Hello and thank you for your strange offer.

(She stops typing but continues to speak as if she is composing an email.)

SUGAR. I'm trying to finish a book. My husband is an artist, we have two kids and ten mountains of debt. I can't take on...

Yeah, I'm in.

(She presses Send.)

LETTER WRITER #1. That's great! I'll forward you the letters.

*(**LETTER WRITER #1** sends the emails from his phone, exits.)*

(Multiple dings of rapidly incoming emails.)

*(**SUGAR** abandons the dishes, takes her computer to the table, sits, and reads.)*

*(**LETTER WRITER #2** enters. **SUGAR** is reading from the computer screen and hears but does not see **LETTER WRITER #2**.)*

Epistles #1

LETTER WRITER #2 & SUGAR. Dear Sugar,

LETTER WRITER #2. I'm jealous of other people's success even if I like them. When my friends get good news I put on a smile but I'm really thinking *why not me*!!

    *(**LETTER WRITER #3** enters.)*

LETTER WRITER #3 & SUGAR. Dear Sugar,

LETTER WRITER #3. I want to make friends and my dad's advice is, just be yourself, but it's not that easy in a new school in eighth grade. Everyone has their own groups. Everyone already knows who they're going to pair up with in science class and I'm stuck with an anti-social kid who picks his nose.

    *(**LETTER WRITER #1** enters.)*

LETTER WRITER #1 & SUGAR. Dear Sugar,

LETTER WRITER #1. I get seasick and I have a boat trip coming up with my boss. He doesn't like me. I mean, he really doesn't like me. I don't want to go on the trip, I want to call in sick before I get on the boat and barf. What's your advice?

LETTER WRITER #2 & SUGAR. Dear Sugar,

LETTER WRITER #2. I'm a seventy-year-old married man and I suspect my newly widowed neighbor is spying on me when I'm in my yard. When I'm out there pulling weeds, to drive her batty, I don't wear a shirt.

LETTER WRITER #1 & SUGAR. Dear Sugar,

LETTER WRITER #1. I am a thirty-five-year-old woman, I lost my job and am entering into an arrangement with a married man: we will rendezvous twice a week and he will pay me $1,000 a month. I have many thoughts and questions, including: is this taxable income?

Like An Iron Bell

LETTER WRITER #3 & SUGAR. Dear Sugar,

LETTER WRITER #3. My question is about love.

(SUGAR *now sees* **LETTER WRITER #3**.)

I'm at the age when most of my friends are married. The closest I've been to the altar was when I was the best man. I've had three relationships. One casual, one serious and one current. There was no issue with the casual one: I was up front about not wanting to settle down. The second one started out casual and I broke it off when she got serious, so I lost both a lover and a friend.

For about four months now, I've been dating another woman. She seems like she's falling in love with me. I avoid that word "love." I don't want to say that word out loud because it comes loaded with promises that are fragile and easily broken. My question is, when do I have to take that big step and say, "I love you"? And, what is this love thing all about, anyway?

Signed,

Confused

SUGAR. Dear Confused...

I agree, that word "love" is highly loaded with – Ah, I agree with you, well that's helpful advice –

Dear Confused...

You certainly must be confused if you're confused – Oh, that's good writing, I will just repeat your word back to you.

Please don't let the timetable by which others live their lives affect yours. No...

Dear Confused,

The last word my mother ever said to me was love. She was forty-five, and so sick and weak she couldn't muster the "I" or the "you," but it didn't matter. That puny word has the power to stand on its own.

I was twenty-two and I wasn't with my mom when she died. No one was. She died alone in a hospital room and for many years it felt like my insides were frozen solid because of that. I ran it over and over in my mind, the choices I made that kept me from being beside my mother in her last hours, but thinking about it didn't do a thing. Thinking about it was a long dive into a bucket of shit that didn't have a bottom.

I would never be with my mother when she died. She would never be alive again. The last thing that happened between us would always be the last thing. There would be the way I got my coat and said, "I love you," and there would be the way she was silent until I was almost out the door and she called:

LETTER WRITER #2. *(As Sugar's mother.) Love.*

> **(SUGAR** *sees* **LETTER WRITER #2** *as her mother in the past.)*

SUGAR. And, there would be the way that she was still lying in that bed when I returned the next morning, but dead.

My mother's last word to me clanks inside me like an iron bell that someone beats at dinnertime:

LETTER WRITER #2. *(As Sugar's mother.) Love, love, love, love, love.*

SUGAR. I'll bet you think this has nothing to do with your question, but your question and my answer are about *love*.

Love is the feeling we have for people we care about and hold in high regard. It can be light as the hug we give a friend or heavy as the sacrifices we make for our children. It can be fleeting, everlasting, conditional, unconditional, stoked by sex, sullied by abuse, nourished by humor.

The point is, you get to define it, you get to describe the oh-wow-I-didn't-mean-to-fall-in-love-but-I-sorta-did love you appear to have for this woman. You've convinced yourself that withholding one small word from her will shield you from getting hurt.

You asked me, when do you have to take that big step and tell your girlfriend that you love her, and my answer is: when you think you love her.

Be brave. Brave enough to break your own heart. Tackle the motherfucking shit out of love. Look, we're all going to die. Hit the iron bell like it's dinnertime.

Signed,
Sugar

Epistles #1A

LETTER WRITER #2. Dear Sugar, Something is different. Who the hell are you?

SUGAR. Hi, I'm the new Sugar –

LETTER WRITER #3. I knew it! Who are you?

LETTER WRITER #2. What's your real name?

SUGAR. Let's keep it at Sugar.

LETTER WRITER #1. Do you write other things?

SUGAR. Yes.

LETTER WRITER #2. Are you a published author?

SUGAR. Yes.

LETTER WRITER #3. As in author of a real book, or a blog?

SUGAR. I have published some things including a novel.

LETTER WRITER #3. So, do you write the letters for the column?

SUGAR. No.

LETTER WRITER #2. Wait, the letters are real?

SUGAR. Yes.

LETTER WRITER #3. All of them?

SUGAR. Yes.

LETTER WRITER #2. Do you have an office, is this your job?

SUGAR. No, I write at home, at night, when I'm supposed to be working on my next book.

LETTER WRITER #1. Have you ever written an advice column before?

SUGAR. No.

LETTER WRITER #3. Are any questions off limits?

SUGAR. No.

LETTER WRITER #1. Do you like it up the ass?

SUGAR. No.

LETTER WRITER #3. Can we really ask you anything?

SUGAR. Yes.

LETTER WRITER #3. What is your name?

SUGAR. Sugar.

LETTER WRITER #1. Dear Sugar, What the fuck, what the fuck, what the fuck? I'm asking this question as it applies to everything every day. Best. WTF.

(**SUGAR** *looks at* **LETTER WRITER #1.**)

How You Get Unstuck

LETTER WRITER #2. Dear Sugar,

I got pregnant, and my boyfriend and me – we were excited to become parents.

When I was six-and-a-half months pregnant, I miscarried.

(SUGAR turns to LETTER WRITER #2.)

Since then, not a day has gone by when I haven't thought about who that child would have been. A girl. She had a name. Every day I wake up and think, "My daughter would be six months old," or, "My daughter would maybe have started crawling today." Sometimes, all I can think is the word *daughter*, *daughter* over and over and over.

I'm not sad or pissed off. I just don't care about anything. I'm numb. And I can't get past it. Most of the people in my life expect me to have moved on by now. One pointed out, "It was only a miscarriage." So I also feel guilty about being so stuck, grieving for a child that never was.

Then there is the reason I lost the baby. My doctor said it was because I was overweight. Part of me thinks the doctor was an asshole for saying that, but another part of me believes that this was my fault. Sometimes, I don't eat for days and then sometimes, I eat everything in sight and throw it all up. I spend hours at the gym, walking on the treadmill until I can't lift my legs.

The rational part of me understands that if I don't pull myself out of this, I'll do serious damage to myself. I know this, and yet I just don't care. I want to know how to care again.

Signed,
Stuck

SUGAR. Dear Stuck,

Some people think they're being honest with you. Others are scared of the intensity of your loss. None of them will be helpful to you. They live on Planet Earth. You live on Planet My Baby Died.

There are many women who have spent their days silently chanting *daughter, daughter* or *son, son* to themselves. You need to find those women. They're your tribe. The healing power of even the most microscopic exchange with someone who knows in a flash precisely what you're talking about because she experienced that thing too cannot be over-estimated.

Several years ago I worked with at-risk girls in middle school. Most of them were poor, white, in seventh or eighth grade.

> (**SUGAR** *turns to the audience and addresses them.*)

My job title was *youth advocate.*

My mission was to help the girls succeed. Succeeding meant not getting pregnant or locked up before graduating high school. It meant eventually holding down a job. It was such a small thing and yet it was enormous. It was like trying to push an eighteen-wheeler with your pinkie finger.

I was scared of them at first. They were thirteen and I was twenty-eight. They hated everything and everything was boring and stupid and either –

SUGAR, LETTER WRITER #1 & LETTER WRITER #3. Totally cool –

SUGAR. Or –

SUGAR, LETTER WRITER #1 & LETTER WRITER #3. Totally gay –

SUGAR. And I had to tell them why not to say the word gay to mean stupid and they thought I was a –

SUGAR, LETTER WRITER #1 & LETTER WRITER #3. Total fag –

SUGAR. For thinking by gay they meant *gay* and then I had to tell them not to say fag and then I passed around journals I'd purchased for them.

LETTER WRITER #1. Do we get to keep these?

> (**SUGAR** *addresses* **LETTER WRITER #1** *and* **#3.**)

SUGAR. Yes. Open them.

> (**SUGAR** *addresses the audience.*)

I asked them each to write down three true things about themselves and one lie and then we read them out loud, guessing which one was the lie. By the time we were halfway around the room they all loved me intensely.

Not me. But how I held them: with unconditional positive regard.

We went to places they'd never been: to a rock-climbing gym and the ballet. I hoped, if they witnessed the grace of live art, they wouldn't steal someone's wallet and go to jail. As they pulled themselves up a fake boulder, they'd start valuing their bodies and would not get knocked up.

Their dads were in prison or unknown to them or fucking them, their moms were strung out on drugs or on the streets. The girls told me ghastly, merciless stories of sorrow and betrayal.

One girl wore an enormous hooded sweatshirt that went down to her knees with the hood pulled up over her head. Across her face hung a dense curtain of hair. It looked like she had two backs of a head and no face. She told me that she slept most nights –

> (**SUGAR** *turns to* **LETTER WRITER #3.**)

LETTER WRITER #3. In a falling down wooden shed near the alley behind the apartment building –

SUGAR. Where she lived. She did this because she –

LETTER WRITER #3. Couldn't take staying inside –

> (**SUGAR** *addresses the audience.*)

SUGAR. Where her mother ranted and raved, alcoholic and mentally ill. Another girl told me that when her mom's boyfriend got mad he –

(SUGAR turns to LETTER WRITER #1.)

LETTER WRITER #1. Dragged me into the yard and turned on the hose and held my face up to the ice cold running water until I almost drowned and then he locked me outside for two hours.

(SUGAR addresses the audience.)

SUGAR. I told the girls that these things were unacceptable. Illegal. That I would call someone and that this would stop. I called the police, I called child protection services. And no one did anything.

So I told the girls something different.

(SUGAR addresses LETTER WRITER #1 and #3.)

This will not stop. It will go on so you have to find a place within yourself to not only escape the shit, but to transcend it, and if you aren't able to do that, then your whole life will be shit, forever and ever and ever. You have to do more than hold on. You have to *reach.*

(SUGAR addresses LETTER WRITER #2.)

And the same is true for you, Stuck, and for anyone who has ever had anything terrible happen to them. How you get unstuck is: you reach. Therapy and speaking with friends and support groups will help, don't hold it inside, get it out, talk it out, cry it out but know this. Nobody else can make this right for you. You have to reach for your desire to heal.

True healing is a fierce place. It's a giant place, a place of monstrous beauty and glimmering light, and you have to work really hard to get there.

(SUGAR addresses the audience.)

Years after I left that job, I was having lunch at a Taco Bell. Just as I was gathering my things to leave, a woman wearing a Taco Bell uniform approached me and said my name. It was the faceless girl who'd lived in the falling down shed. Her hair was pulled back into a ponytail now. She was grown up.

(**SUGAR** *turns to* **LETTER WRITER #3**.)

LETTER WRITER #3. Hey.

SUGAR. Is that you?

LETTER WRITER #3. I made it. Didn't I?

SUGAR. You did. You absolutely did.

(**SUGAR** *addresses* **LETTER WRITER #2**.)

Signed,
Sugar

A Motorcycle With No One On It

(**LETTER WRITER #1** *approaches* **SUGAR.**)

LETTER WRITER #1. Dear Sugar,

I'm middle-aged, married and crushing on a friend. And it's full-blown, just like in high school, sweaty palms, distracted, giddy, the whole shebang. If we'd met at a different time we'd probably be together.

We spend hours talking. We're never bored. We can't stop smiling around each other. We really like each other.

So far it has gone no farther than flirting. We've never kissed. We've never crossed a physical boundary. But we *really* like each other.

My question isn't what should I do – I'm pretty clear I should behave and I want to behave, I really want to – but what should I do?

Signed,

Crushed

SUGAR. Dear Crushed,

That's...basically every middle-aged married person. X is married to Y but wants to fuck Z.

Because Z is new and is never going to bitch at you for forgetting to take out the trash. Z doesn't even care that you were late, 'cause Z doesn't wear a watch.

Z is like a motorcycle with no one on it. Dazzling. Going nowhere.

Signed,

Sugar

The Truth That Lives There

LETTER WRITER #2. Dear Sugar,

The thought of staying in my marriage makes me feel panicky and claustrophobic. My wife and I have some things in common, but I don't feel like those are enough. I find myself fantasizing about dating other people. I'm afraid I will get more bored as time goes on. I'm also afraid that there is no one better out there for me that I should be grateful for what I have.

LETTER WRITER #3. Dear Sugar,

I want to leave my marriage but I don't want to embarrass her, I'm terrified of hurting her. She has been so good to me and I consider her my best friend. I think I love her but I'm not in love with her.

LETTER WRITER #1. Dear Sugar,

I feel trapped and like I'm hiding the real me. I don't blame him for my discontent. But I never wanted to get married and now I don't know how to stop this charade. I want out, but how?

LETTER WRITER #3. Signed,

Afraid to Leave

LETTER WRITER #2. Signed,

I Can't Do This

LETTER WRITER #1. Signed,

How Can I Hurt Him?

SUGAR. Dear All of Us Who Want to Please,

There was nothing wrong with my first husband. He wasn't perfect, but he was pretty close. I met him a month after I turned nineteen and I married him on a rash and romantic impulse a month before I turned twenty.

But there was in me an awful thing, from almost the very beginning: a small, clear voice that would not, no matter what I did, would not stop saying *go*.

Go, even though you love him.

Go, even though he's kind and faithful and dear to you.

Go, even though he's your best friend and you're his.

Go, even though your friends will be disappointed or surprised or pissed off or all three.

Go, even though you once said you would stay.

Go, even though you're afraid of being alone.

Go, even though there is nowhere to go.

Go, because you want to.

Because wanting to leave is enough.

Get a pen. Write that last sentence on your palm. Then read it over and over again until your tears have washed it away.

When it came to my first marriage, I tried to be good. I tried to be bad. I was sad and scared and self-sacrificing and ultimately self-destructive. I finally cheated on my former husband because I didn't have the guts to tell him I wanted out. I loved him too much to make a clean break, so I botched the job and made it dirty instead. Divorcing him was the most excruciating decision I ever made. But I wasn't the only one whose life was better. He deserved the love of a woman who didn't have the word –

LETTER WRITER #2 & SUGAR. "Go"–

SUGAR. Whispering like a deranged ghost in her ear. We all know when we –

LETTER WRITER #3 & SUGAR. Need to –

LETTER WRITER #1 & SUGAR. Want to –

LETTER WRITER #2 & SUGAR. Must...go.

SUGAR. I only ask: will you do it later or will you do it now?

Signed,
Sugar

Epistles #2

LETTER WRITER #2. Dear Sugar,

We still don't know who the hell you are and seriously, who the hell do you think you are? This week you're telling people to leave their marriages? Last week it was the opposite: you said don't have an affair; you said don't be X fucking Z or you'll turn into a motorcycle! What are you trying to make us do?

Signed,

Not Buying It

SUGAR. Dear Not Buying It,

My goal isn't to make anyone do anything, I'm offering advice based on my personal experiences.

LETTER WRITER #1. Oh wow, did you just make this about you?

LETTER WRITER #3. Are you a therapist?

SUGAR. No.

LETTER WRITER #1. Are you *in* therapy?

SUGAR. No.

LETTER WRITER #3. Are you even qualified for this gig?

LETTER WRITER #2. Dear Sugar,

Your advice is all over the place! How can you suggest in one column that we stick to convention and then in the very next one say that we gotta be bold?! Make up your mind. Whatever. Why am I trying to figure out who you are, do you even know who you are? Make a choice. Pick a lane.

Signed,

Still Not Buying It

SUGAR. Dear Still Not Buying It,

Years ago I was in a café with the man who is now my husband. We'd only been lovers for a month, but we were already in deep, thick in the thrall of the you-tell-me-everything-and-I'll-tell-you-everything-because-I-love-you-so-madly stage. On this day, I was telling him about my divorce, then my months of heroin use which led to the tale of how I'd gotten pregnant by a heroin addict and how I'd felt so angry about having an abortion that I'd intentionally sliced a line in my arm with a knife. He stopped me. He said,

LETTER WRITER #3. *(As Mr. Sugar.)* Don't get me wrong.

> *(SUGAR sees Mr. Sugar as he was in the past.)*

I want to hear everything about your life. But I want you to know that you don't need to tell me this to get me to love you. You don't have to be broken for me.

> *(SUGAR addresses LETTER WRITER #2.)*

SUGAR. I remember that moment precisely. It wasn't a good feeling. I had never realized that I thought to get a man to love me I had to appear to be broken for him. But when he said it, I recognized it. Here was a man – a good, kind, compassionate man – finally calling me out.

LETTER WRITER #3. *(As Mr. Sugar.)* You don't have to be broken for me.

SUGAR. I didn't have to be broken for him, even though parts of me were.

I realized I could be every piece of myself. I could be vulnerable and strong, fearful and fearless, I could be everything I was and wanted to be. And that things could be valid and yet contradictions of each other was the unification of the ancient and the future parts of me.

And within that moment, I was open, I was bare.

I will be open with you. I will be bare. I will show you my brokenness and my strengths and I will do my best to offer my best, tough, sweet and even occasionally contradicting advice. I don't know if my unorthodox approach is wrong or right.

Sure, advice columnists are supposed to position themselves as The Ones Who Know but I'm not that person; I am The One Who Doesn't Know But Who Will Work Really Really Hard To See What I Can Find. This is who I am. Tell me, who are you?

Signed…

Yours,
Sugar

Epistles #3

LETTER WRITER #1. Dear Sugar –

LETTER WRITER #3. Dear Sugar –

LETTER WRITER #2. Dear Sugar –

LETTER WRITER #1. Dear Sugar, I was in an accident that injured my spine and now I'm secretly addicted to pain meds.

LETTER WRITER #3. Dear Sugar, I'm afraid of my violent older brother who has terrorized me since we were kids.

LETTER WRITER #2. Dear Sugar, Icky thoughts turn me on. I have repulsive thoughts of men taking me aggressively and my being submissive to them in bed.

LETTER WRITER #1. Dear Sugar, My wife drinks while I'm at work and when I get home she thinks I can't tell.

LETTER WRITER #3. Dear Sugar, My daughter has a tumor and is having brain surgery tomorrow and I find myself doubting God's existence.

LETTER WRITER #2. Dear Sugar, My birth mother doesn't want to meet me.

LETTER WRITER #1. Dear Sugar, What the fuck, what the fuck, what the fuck? I'm asking this question as it applies to everything every day. Best, WTF.

(**SUGAR** *looks at* **LETTER WRITER #1.**)

On Your Island

LETTER WRITER #3. Dear Sugar,

I'm thirty-four years old and I'm transgender.

(**SUGAR** *turns to* **LETTER WRITER #3.**)

I was born a female but I knew I was meant to be male for as long as I can remember. I had the usual painful childhood and adolescence in a smallish town because I was different – picked on by other kids, misunderstood by my family.

Seven years ago I told my mom and dad I intended to have sex reassignment surgery.* They were furious. They said the worst things you can imagine anyone saying to another human being, especially if that human being is your child. In response, I cut off ties with them, moved away and made a new life living as a man. I have friends and romance in my life. I love my job. I'm happy with who I've become and the life I've made.

After years of no contact, I got an email from my parents that blew my mind. They apologized. They were sorry they never understood and now they do. They said they miss me and they love me. Sugar, they want me back.

I cried like crazy and that surprised me. I believed I didn't love my parents anymore.

I have made it without them. I've created an island far away and safe from my past. I made it because I'm tough. Do I forgive them and get back in touch, or do I ignore their email and stay safe on my island? What do I do?

Signed,
Orphan

---

*Licensees can replace "sex reassignment surgery" with "gender confirmation surgery" if they so choose. It is the author's hope that licensees will rehearse both options and choose whichever feels best.

SUGAR. Dear Orphan,

Forgive your parents. Not for them. For you. You've remade yourself. You and your mom and dad can remake this too – the new era in which they are finally capable of loving the authentic you.

What they did to you seven years ago is terrible. They now know that. Here's the difference between your parents and so many other parents who have tried to remain in their children's lives after a time of abuse or trauma. They're sorry. They're more sorry than most.

Your parents have grown and changed and come to understand things that confounded them before. Refusing to accept them for the people they are isn't any different from them refusing to accept you for who you are. It's not tough, it's weak.

You've had to ask yourself impossible questions, endure humiliations, and redefine your life in ways that most people can't even imagine.

But you know what? So have your parents.

When you needed them, they were drowning in their own fear.

They aren't drowning anymore, they swam to shore.

They have arrived at last on your island.

Welcome them.

Yours,
Sugar

I Chose Van Gogh

LETTER WRITER #2. Dear Sugar,

Four years ago, I was raped.

Anger and panic became a deep part of my life and almost dragged me under. It took a long time but I pulled myself up and onward.

I feel it's behind me and I am over it.

Well, I have been dating a great guy for about a year and a half, we have a healthy and positive relationship.

Do I tell him about my sexual assault?

Do I need to?

We've been through some stuff but I don't know if he's capable of hearing about this.

I worry it might freak him out and affect our relationship.

I need your advice.

Signed,
Why Tell?

SUGAR. Dear Why Tell,

I asked my friend, a talented painter, how she recovered from being sexually assaulted, how she resumed having healthy sexual relationships with men, how she continued to go on and be a talented painter and live a full life. She told me that we get to decide who we allow to influence us.

She said, "I could allow myself to be influenced by a man who screwed me against my will or I could allow myself to be influenced by van Gogh.

I chose van Gogh."

You chose van Gogh too. I salute you for making your way through your experience to this side of it.

But you have a secret within you.

Keeping this trauma from your boyfriend doesn't let him know what a warrior you are.

We need to let the people who love us see what made us.

Tell your boyfriend about your sexual assault. What happened. How you suffered. How you made your way through it. How you feel about it now. Tell him. Otherwise it creates the burden of a secret you are too wonderful to keep.

Yours,
Sugar

The Ordinary Miraculous

LETTER WRITER #3. Dear Sugar,

> One of the general mysteries of life is that I don't know what something will turn out to be until I've lived through it. Will you give us an example of something you thought was one thing, and then became another?
>
> Signed,
> Curious

SUGAR. Dear Curious,

> The summer I was eighteen, I was driving down a country road with my mother when we stopped at a yard sale. There was nothing much of interest at the sale, but a moment before I was about to suggest we leave, something caught my eye: a red velvet dress trimmed with white lace, fit for a toddler.
>
> I was pretty certain at that moment that I would never be a mother myself. Children were fine but ultimately annoying. I wanted more out of life. And yet, ridiculously, inexplicably I wanted that red dress. Something about it called powerfully to me. My mother picked it up.

LETTER WRITER #2. *(As Sugar's mother.)* You want this dress? For someday?

> *(**SUGAR** sees **LETTER WRITER #2** as her mother in the past.)*

SUGAR. But I'm not even going to have kids…

LETTER WRITER #2. *(As Sugar's mother.)* You can put it in a box. Then you'll have it, no matter what you decide.

SUGAR. I don't have a dollar.

LETTER WRITER #2. I do.

> *(**SUGAR** addresses the audience.)*

SUGAR. Three years later, I'd be standing in a field not far from that yard sale, holding the ashes of my mother's body in my palms. My mother was gone, the red dress was still with me, packed into a cedar box that had belonged to her. I dragged it with me all the way along the scorching trail of my twenties and into my thirties, when I had two children: a son and then a daughter. The red dress was a secret only known by me, buried for years among my mother's best things. When I unearthed it and held it again it was like being slapped and kissed at the same time, like the volume was being turned way up and also way down. The two things that were true about its existence had an opposite effect and were yet the same single fact:

My mother bought a dress for the granddaughter she'll never know.

My mother bought a dress for the granddaughter she'll never know.

How beautiful. How ugly.

How little. How big.

How painful. How sweet.

It's seldom that we can draw a direct line between this and that. My desire to buy the dress was made meaningful only by my mother's death and my daughter's birth. The dress was the material evidence of my loss, but also of the way my mother's love had carried me forth beyond her, her life extending years into my own in ways I never could have imagined in the moment the red dress caught my eye. And seeing my daughter on the second Christmas of her life wearing the dress the grandmother she'd never meet bought for her, returned something to me that I thought had been lost forever.

We cannot possibly know what will manifest in our lives. We live and have experiences and leave people we love and get left by them. People we thought would be with us forever aren't and people we didn't know would come into our lives do. Our work here is to keep faith with that, to put it in a box and wait. To trust that someday we will know what it means, so that when the ordinary miraculous is revealed to us we will be there, standing before the baby girl in the pretty dress, grateful for the smallest things.

Yours,
Sugar

Epistles #4

LETTER WRITER #2. Dear Sugar –

LETTER WRITER #1. Dear Sugar –

LETTER WRITER #3. Dear Sugar –

LETTER WRITER #2. Dear Sugar –

LETTER WRITER #1. Dear Sugar –

LETTER WRITER #3. Dear Sugar –

LETTER WRITER #2. Dear Sugar, If it's true that drug addicts stop maturing at the time they started using, then the same thing happens at weddings!

LETTER WRITER #1. Dear Sugar, I am worried I will die alone.

LETTER WRITER #3. Dear Sugar, When it comes to holding down a job, I'm the worst.

LETTER WRITER #2. Dear Sugar, I think I'm attracted to my teacher.

LETTER WRITER #1. Dear Sugar, Are you there?

LETTER WRITER #2. Dear Sugar, Where are you?

LETTER WRITER #3. Dear Sugar, Why aren't you answering me?

LETTER WRITER #2. Dear Sugar, My roommate is selfish. Are you ever going to answer me?

Sexy Santa

LETTER WRITER #1. Dear Sugar,

Kind of crazy, but my girlfriend is seriously turned on by Santa Claus. The old dude, big belly, white beard, his power to find out if you're naughty or nice. The whole thing just gets her going. It's our first Christmas together. She told me about the fantasy when Santa started to pop up all over the place. She gets especially turned on when she sees an actual Santa, which starts her thinking about sitting in his lap and what could happen next. You get the picture.

So here's my question. My sister has two young sons. A few years ago, she bought a Santa suit and I've been dressing up in it and going over to her place to give my nephews a thrill on Christmas Eve.

Anyway...it occurred to me that if I keep the suit for a bit I can give my girlfriend a thrill too. Creepy? Good idea? Bad idea? What do you make of this plan?

Thanks.

Sexy Santa

SUGAR. Dear Sexy Santa...

Your giving spirit is genuinely what the holiday season is all about! I say, stuff that woman's stocking the way only Santa knows how.

Yours,

Sugar

Known Unknowns

LETTER WRITER #3. Dear Sugar,

I dated this girl for a while until I realized she was self-absorbed, so I dumped her. And, she became another one of my crazy exes. Then, she had a fight with her best friend, they stopped being friends. That ex-best friend of my ex called me up to hang out. I ended up banging her.

A few days later, she tells me she's engaged. She wears this weird short-haired wig while she breaks up with me. The thing is, I connected better with her in the three days we hung out than I did with my ex in months. Please help me figure out what I should do now, which woman I should be with. I'm not a smart man but I do know what love is.

Signed,

Gump

SUGAR. Dear Gump,

I keep politics out of this column. But just this once, let's recall when former Secretary of Defense Donald Rumsfeld quite wisely said something like:

"There are known knowns. These are the things we know we know.

And, there are known unknowns. These are the things we know we do not know.

But there are also unknown unknowns, these are the things we do not know we do not know."

When it comes to your triangular quagmire, let's start with the known knowns. These are the things you know you know.

A:

LETTER WRITER #3. I didn't want to fuck my girlfriend anymore so I broke up with her.

SUGAR. B:

LETTER WRITER #3. I fucked my ex-girlfriend's ex-best friend for three days, things were good.

SUGAR. C:

LETTER WRITER #3. She put on a wig and told me she didn't want to fuck me anymore.

SUGAR. Which brings us to the known unknowns, the things you know you do not know. A:

LETTER WRITER #3. How come so many of my exes are crazy?

SUGAR. B:

LETTER WRITER #3. Is my ex-girlfriend's ex-best friend really engaged to be married or is she trying to shake me?

SUGAR. C:

LETTER WRITER #3. Why the wig?

SUGAR. Which brings us to the unknown unknowns, the things that you don't know you don't know.

A) You don't have a future with either of these women.

B) Neither is even thinking about you.

C) And yet: You are loved. You wrote to me with your scared, searching, knuckle-headed heart on full display. It takes a lot to be that brave. And you are. So I love you. And, the only advice I have for you is: go find another girlfriend.

Yours,

Sugar

Epistles #4A

LETTER WRITER #2. Dear Sugar, My sister has been in hospice care for six months.

LETTER WRITER #3. Dear Sugar, He said he only hired me because he is attracted to me.

LETTER WRITER #2. Dear Sugar, My two sons ages thirty-five and thirty-one have returned to the nest, my home. They didn't ask.

LETTER WRITER #3. Dear Sugar, I was born with a rare blood disorder that has left me with physical deformities.

LETTER WRITER #1. Dear Sugar, What the fuck? What the fuck? What the fuck? I'm asking this question as it applies to everything every day. Best, WTF.

The Baby Bird

SUGAR. Dear WTF,

My father's father made me jack him off when I was three and four and five. I wasn't any good at it. My hands were too small and I couldn't get the rhythm right and I didn't understand what I was doing. I only knew I didn't want to do it. Knew that it made me feel miserable and anxious in a way so sickeningly particular that I can feel that same particular sickness rising this very moment in my throat. I hated having to rub my grandfather's cock, but there was nothing I could do. I *had* to do it. My grandfather babysat my sister and me a couple times a week and most of the days that I was trapped in his house with him he would pull his already-getting-hard penis out of his pants and say *come here* and that was that.

I moved far away from him when I was nearly six and soon after that my parents split up and my father left my life and I never saw my grandfather again. He died of black lung disease when he was sixty-six and I was fifteen. When I learned he died, I wasn't sad. I wasn't happy either. He was no one to me and yet he was always there, the force of him and what he'd made me do moving through me like a dark river. For years, I didn't say a word about it to anyone. I hoped silence would make it disappear. But it didn't.

So I railed against it, in search of the answer to what the fuck was up with my grandfather doing that to me. But I could never shake it. That particular fuck would not be shook. Asking what the fuck only brought it around. Around and around it went, my grandfather's cock in my hands, the memory of it so vivid, so *palpable*, so very much a part of me. It came to me during sex and not during sex. It came to me in flashes and it came to me in dreams. It came to me one day when I found a baby bird that had fallen from a nest.

I'd always heard that you're not supposed to pick up baby birds; that once you touch them their mama won't come back and get them, but it doesn't matter if that's true or not. I knew there was only one humane thing to do. I put the baby bird in a paper bag and smothered it with my hands.

Nothing that has died in my life has ever died easily and this bird was no exception. I could feel it through the paper bag, pulsing against my hand and rearing up, simultaneously flaccid and ferocious beneath its translucent sheen of skin, precisely as my grandfather's cock had been.

There it was! There it was again. The ghost of that old man's cock would always be in my hands. But I understood what I was doing this time. I understood that I had to press harder than I could bear. It *had* to die. Pressing harder was murder. It was mercy.

That's what the fuck it was. The fuck was mine.

And the fuck is yours too. That question does not apply to "everything every day." If it does, you're wasting your life. If it does, you are a lazy coward and you are not a lazy coward. Ask better questions. The fuck is your life. Answer it.

Yours,
Sugar

The Empty Bowl

LETTER WRITER #3. Dear Sugar,

My father is a narcissist: controlling, vain, volatile, and charming. If I wasn't cheerful enough, I was locked in my room for days; if I made a joke he'd yell and curse at me. My father would denounce me as his child over slight disagreements. When he decided that everything was fine again, I was expected to accept his change of heart – no apologies offered (unless they were mine). I could never be perfect enough, and yet I tried so hard to make him proud, to make him care. He was my dad after all.

Still now, as an adult, it's not better. He is so consumed by his image that when he found out that my therapist – an understanding, kind, and sympathetic counselor – was a woman he knew, he insisted I stop seeing her.

But three months ago he went too far. He betrayed my mother, and I was a fucking bitch for finding out about his infidelity.

People insist that family is important, that it is my duty to forgive the man that gave me life and to keep him in my life. He's the only father that I have. But is it worth the pain?

Signed,

When is too much too much?

SUGAR. Dear Too Much,

No, maintaining a relationship with your abusive father is not worth it. Yes, he is the only father you will ever have, but that does not give him the right to abuse you. The standard you should apply in deciding whether or not to have an active relationship with him is the same one you should apply to all the relationships in your life: you will not be mistreated or disrespected or manipulated.

Your father does not currently meet that standard.

My mother left my father because he'd been violent and abusive. I haven't had parents as an adult, and yet I carry them with me every day. They are like two empty bowls I've had to repeatedly fill on my own. I think your father will have the same effect on you. Even if you cut off ties with your dad, you won't fully escape him, he will be the empty bowl that you will have to fill again and again.

After my mother died, I wrote a letter to my dad saying that, for me to have a relationship with him, he first had to explain why he'd done the things he'd done. He didn't write back.

Seventeen years passed.

Then one day the phone rang and there it was: my father's name on the screen of my telephone.

LETTER WRITER #1. *(As Sugar's father.)* Hello…

> (**SUGAR** *sees* **LETTER WRITER #1** *as her father in the past.)*

SUGAR. Hello…

LETTER WRITER #1. *(As Sugar's father.)* Do you watch Rachael Ray?

SUGAR. Rachael Ray?

LETTER WRITER #1. *(As Sugar's father.)* Rachael Ray, you know. The cookbook writer. She has a talk show.

SUGAR. Uh, yeah…

> (**SUGAR** *addresses the audience.)*

And on it went, the most flabbergasting conversation I've ever had. My father spoke to me as if we spoke every week, as if nothing that had happened had happened, as if my entire childhood did not exist. The topics were recipes, poodles, cataracts, sunscreen. I got off the phone fifteen minutes later, utterly bewildered. He wasn't ill or delusional. He was my father, talking to me as if I was his daughter. As if he had a right.

But he didn't.

For all those years without him in my life, I always thought of my dad on my birthday. How, on the day I was born, he must have held me in his hands and thought his baby was a miracle. He must have believed he could be a better person than he'd been before.

(**SUGAR** *addresses* **LETTER WRITER #3**.)

A few days after that phone call, he sent me a chatty note over email. When I replied I said what I'd said in the letter I'd written to him seventeen years before – that I would consider having a relationship with him only after we had spoken about our shared past. He replied inquiring what it was I "wanted to know."

I wrote the most loving, painful and forgiving letter of my life. Then I pressed *send*.

My father's reply came so quickly it seemed impossible that he'd read the whole thing. In enraged words he wrote that I should never contact him again and that he was glad to be finally rid of me.

I didn't cry. I laced on my running shoes and went out my front door and walked through my neighborhood to a park and up a big hill. I didn't stop walking until I got all the way to the top and then I sat down on a bench that looked over the city.

I had that feeling you get – there is no word for this feeling – when you are simultaneously happy and sad and angry and grateful and accepting and appalled and every other possible emotion, all smashed together and amplified. Why is there no word for this feeling? I sat for so long on that bench looking at the sky and the land and the trees, thinking: my father – *my father!* – he is finally, finally, finally rid of me.

Perhaps *healing* is the word and we don't want to believe that. We want to believe the word healing is more pure and perfect, like a baby on its birthday. And when we're holding it in our hands, we'll be better people than we'd been before. Like we have to be.

Yours,
Sugar

Epistles #5

*(**SUGAR** and the **LETTER WRITERS** gather in the kitchen. Using items in the refrigerator and her surroundings, **SUGAR** makes two childrens' lunches.)*

LETTER WRITER #2. Dear Sugar, Do you ever read the comments after you've posted a response to a letter?

SUGAR. I'm a writer posting things online so I try to avoid reading the comments...yes, I read all the comments.

LETTER WRITER #1. I wanted to tell you that I had this hot dream about you even though I don't know what you look like, if your hair is straight or curly, if you're curvy or skinny, but it didn't matter because you were woman and we were getting down.

SUGAR. Okay.

LETTER WRITER #2. C'mon, who are you, Sugar?! It's making me crazy. I want to know! What would a photograph of you look like?

SUGAR. A woman standing naked in the light of day. She's flawed, but okay with that. Her hands are obscuring her face. You see everything but one thing.

LETTER WRITER #1. Why can't we see that one thing, why can't we see your face and know who you are?

SUGAR. You know who I am, I reveal myself to you in every column.

LETTER WRITER #3. If you had to give one piece of advice to people in their twenties, what would it be?

SUGAR. Be about ten times more generous than you believe yourself capable of being.

LETTER WRITER #1. Why?

SUGAR. Because in your twenties you're becoming who you're going to be, so you might as well not become an asshole.

LETTER WRITER #2. What's something weird that happened to you?

SUGAR. Something weird... One time I was hiking up a mountain, on a trail with a little snow in some places, in New Mexico. There was no one around for hours until I met two people – a man and a woman who had just met each other. We were three strangers who met on a mountain. We got to talking and found out that we all had the same birthday and not only that, we were born in three consecutive years. As we were talking, three feathers blew up to us on the snow. We picked them up. That was weird.

LETTER WRITER #3. Can you please tell us some of the dumb things you've done?

SUGAR. Heroin. Meth. The withdrawal method. A blow job by a lake. An idiot punk at a Beastie Boys concert.

LETTER WRITER #2. What's a piece of advice you've given that's taken you some time to learn?

SUGAR. If the word *forgiveness* is written on one side of a coin, on the other side of that coin is written the word *no*. No is golden. It's the good kind of power. It's the way emotionally evolved people live their lives. It's the way to set boundaries. No means you're choosing what to share.

LETTER WRITER #3. Will you tell us your name?

SUGAR. No.

LETTER WRITER #2. Will you ever tell us your name?

SUGAR. Yes.

LETTER WRITER #1. It doesn't matter to me who you are. Where did you get that big heart of yours?

SUGAR. From my mother. From my father. From a crack in the sidewalk where a flower grew. From the blow job by the lake. From the lake. From saying yes to strange offers. From all of you.

(**SUGAR** *places the lunches in the fridge.*)

The Bad Things You Did

LETTER WRITER #2. Dear Sugar,

For many years I stole compulsively. I blame myself, even though I was on a "cocktail" of psychotropic drugs for depression, anxiety and insomnia. I stole a pair of jeans from a friend, flower pots from a neighbor, money from a girlfriend's wallet. I blame myself even though I grew up with my abusive mother screaming at me that I was a liar, a cheat, and a thief. I was not only trying to fulfill my mother's prophecy, but maybe trying to get people to hate and reject me for being a liar, a cheat and a thief.

I hate myself, loathe myself for what I've done. I wonder if I should confess to the friends who will surely reject me. Sugar, can I forgive myself without admitting to people how I wronged them? Please help.

Signed,
Thief

SUGAR. Dear Thief,

On a warm spring day several years ago, I saw I was down to my last twenty cents. So I put nearly everything I owned out on a lawn – my thrift store dresses, my knick-knacks and dishes.

*(**SUGAR** addresses the audience.)*

Customers came and went throughout the day, but my primary companions were a group of eleven-year-old boys who flitted about, inquiring how much this and that cost, even though they didn't have the money to purchase.

Late in the day, they told me one of the boys had stolen something from me – an empty retro leather camera case that I'd once used as a purse. It was a small thing, a barely-worth-bothering-about item that would've sold for only a couple of bucks, but still, I asked the accused boy if he'd taken it.

(**SUGAR** *turns to* **LETTER WRITER #3.**)

LETTER WRITER #3. No.

(**SUGAR** *addresses the audience.*)

SUGAR. The next day he returned wearing a big gray sweatshirt. When he thought I wasn't looking, he pulled the camera case from beneath his shirt and placed it where it had been sitting the day before.

LETTER WRITER #3. Your thing is back.

(**SUGAR** *addresses* **LETTER WRITER #3.**)

SUGAR. Good. Why did you steal it?

LETTER WRITER #3. I didn't.

(**SUGAR** *addresses the audience.*)

SUGAR. It was a sunny day. A few of the boys sat with me on the porch steps, telling me about their lives. The boy who'd stolen my camera case showed me his bicep and insisted in a tone more belligerent than the others that the chains he wore around his neck were real gold.

(**SUGAR** *addresses* **LETTER WRITER #3.**)

Why'd you steal my camera case?

LETTER WRITER #3. I didn't. I just took it while I went to my house to get money.

(**SUGAR** *addresses the audience.*)

SUGAR. The day went by and soon it was just the two of us. He told me about the mother he rarely saw and his much older siblings; about the kind of hot car he was going to buy the instant he turned sixteen.

(**SUGAR** *addresses* **LETTER WRITER #3.**)

Why did you steal my camera case?

LETTER WRITER #3. Because I was lonely.

(**SUGAR** *addresses the audience.*)

SUGAR. There are only a few times anyone has been as self-aware and nakedly honest as that boy was with me in that moment. When he said what he said, I almost fell off the steps. Perhaps because when he told about himself, he told me something about myself. I used to steal things too. I took a compact of blue eye shadow from my cousin, a pretty sweater from a school friend…a figurine of a white dog with its head askew. I didn't know why I stole things and I still can't properly say, but because I was lonely seems about the rightest thing I've ever heard.

(**SUGAR** *addresses* **LETTER WRITER #2.**)

I think you were lonely too. And lonely isn't a crime. I don't think the path to wholeness is walking backward up the trail. The people you stole from don't need you to fess up. But you're so very invested in your self-loathing. If you perpetually condemn yourself for being a liar and thief, does that make you good?

I don't like the thief part of my narrative either. I struggled with whether or not I should talk about it here – it's the first time I've written about it – ever. I've written about all sorts of other "bad things" I've done – promiscuous sex, drugs…this seems worse.

But this is who I am. This is who you are. Can we forgive ourselves?

Years after I stopped stealing, I was sitting alone by a river. I found myself thinking about all the things I'd taken and before I even knew what I was doing I began picking a blade of grass for each one and then dropping it into the water. *I am forgiven* I thought as I let go of the blade that stood in for the blue eye shadow. I am forgiven, I thought for the pretty sweater,

LETTER WRITER #2 & SUGAR. *I am forgiven,*

SUGAR. For the dog figurine and so on until I'd let all the bad things I'd done float right on down the river and I'd said,

LETTER WRITER #2 & SUGAR. *I am forgiven,*

SUGAR. So many times it felt like I actually was.

That doesn't mean I never grappled with it again. You have to say,

LETTER WRITER #2 & SUGAR. *I am forgiven,*

SUGAR. Over and over until it becomes the story you believe about yourself. Every last one of us has the capacity to do that, you included. I hope you will.

I don't know what ever came of that lonely boy at my yard sale. I hope he's made right what was wrong inside of him.

(**SUGAR** *addresses the audience.*)

When I closed down the sale, that camera case he'd stolen from me was still sitting there. I held it out to him.

(**SUGAR** *addresses* **LETTER WRITER #3.**)

You want this?

LETTER WRITER #3. Yes please.

SUGAR. Yours,

(**SUGAR** *addresses* **LETTER WRITER #2.**)

Sugar

The Obliterated Place

LETTER WRITER #1. Dear Sugar,

One.

It's taken me many weeks to compose this letter and even still, I can't do it right. The only way I can get it out is to make a list instead of write a letter.

Two.

I don't have a definite question for you. I'm a sad, angry man whose son died. I want him back. That's all I ask for and it's not a question.

Three.

Nearly four years ago, a drunk driver drove through a red light and hit my son at full speed. The dear boy I loved more than life itself was dead before the paramedics even got to him. He was twenty-two, my only child.

Four.

I'm a father while not being a father. Most days it feels like my grief is going to kill me, or maybe it already has. I'm a living dead dad.

Five.

Your column has helped me go on. I have faith in my version of God and I pray every day and the way I feel when I'm in my deepest prayer is the way I feel when I read your words.

Six.

I see a psychologist regularly and I'm not clinically depressed or on medication.

Seven.

Suicide has occurred to me but I can't do it because it would be a betrayal of my values and also of the values I instilled in my son.

Eight.

I have good friends and family who are supportive and even my ex-wife and I have become close friends again since our son's death.

Nine.

I have a good job and my health.

Ten.

I'm going on with things in a way that makes it appear like I'm adjusting to life without my son, but the fact is I'm living a private hell.

Eleven.

Sometimes the pain is so great I simply lie in my bed and wail.

Twelve.

I can't stop thinking about my son.

Thirteen.

I can't stop thinking about the things my son would be doing now if he were alive and also the things I did with him when he was young.

Fourteen.

I hate the man who killed my son. For his crime, he was incarcerated eighteen months, then released. He wrote me a letter of apology, but I barely scanned it, I ripped it into pieces and threw it in the garbage.

Fifteen.

I fear you will choose not to answer my letter because you haven't lost a child.

Sixteen.

I fear if you choose to answer my letter people will make critical comments about you, saying you don't have the right to speak to this matter because you have not lost a child.

Seventeen.

I pray you will never lose a child.

Eighteen.

I will understand if you choose not to answer my letter. Most people, kind as they are, don't know what to say to me so why should you?

Nineteen.

I'm writing to you because the way you've written about your grief over your mother dying so young has been meaningful to me.

Twenty.

What can you say to me?

Twenty-one.

How do I go on?

Twenty-two.

How do I become human again?

Signed,

Living Dead Dad

SUGAR. Dear Living Dead Dad,

One.

I don't know how you go on without your son. I only know that you do. And you have. And you will.

Two.

Your shattering letter is proof of that.

Three.

You don't need me to tell you how to be human again. You are there, in all of your humanity, shining unimpeachably before every person reading these words right now.

Four.

I am so sorry for your loss. *I am so sorry for your loss.*

Iamsosorryforyourloss.

Five.

You could stitch together a quilt with all the times that that has been and will be said to you. You could make a river of consolation words. But they won't bring your son back. They won't keep that man from getting into his car and careening through that red light at the precise moment your son was in his path.

Six.

You'll never keep that man from getting into that car.

Seven.

When you peel back the rage and you peel back the thoughts of suicide and you peel back the man who got into the car, at the center of that there is your pure father love that is stronger than anything.

Eight.

No one can touch that love or alter it or take it away from you. Your love for your son belongs only to you.

Nine.

Small things have saved me: how much I love my mother – even after all these years. How powerfully I carry her within me. My grief is tremendous but my love is bigger. So is yours. You are not grieving your son's death because his death was ugly and unfair. You're grieving it because you loved him truly. The beauty in that is greater than the bitterness of his death.

Ten.

I keep imagining you lying on your bed and wailing. I keep thinking that hard as it is to do it's time for you to go silent and lift your head from the bed and listen to what's there in the wake of your wail.

Eleven.

It's your life. The one you must make in the obliterated place that's now your world, where everything you used to be is simultaneously erased and omnipresent, where you are forevermore a living dead dad.

Twelve.

A literal translation of the word "obliterate" is being against the letters. It was impossible for you to write me a letter, so you made me a list instead.

Thirteen.

The obliterated place is equal parts destruction and creation. The obliterated place is pitch black and it is bright light. It is water and it is parched earth. It is mud and it is manna. The work of deep grief is making a home there.

Fourteen.

More will be revealed. Your son hasn't yet taught you everything he has to teach you. He taught you how to love like you've never loved before. He taught you how to suffer like you've never suffered before. Perhaps the next thing he has to teach you is acceptance. And the thing after that, forgiveness.

Fifteen.

Forgiveness bellows from the bottom of the canoe. There are stories you'll learn if you're strong enough to travel there. One of them might cure you.

Sixteen.

We say, "I can't go on," instead of saying we hope we won't have to. You have the power to withstand this sorrow. We all do.

Seventeen.

You go on by doing the best you can. You go on by being generous. You go on by offering comfort to others who can't go on. You go on by allowing the unbearable days to pass and allowing the pleasure in other days. You go on by finding a channel for your rage and another for your love.

Eighteen.

When my son was six, he said people die at all ages. He said it without fear or anguish. It has been healing to me to accept in a very simple way that my mother's life was forty-five years long, that there was nothing beyond that.

Nineteen.

When you say you experience my writing as sacred, what you are touching is the place within me that is my mother. Sugar is the temple I built in my obliterated place. I'd give it all back, but the fact is, my grief taught me things. It required me to suffer. It compelled me to reach.

Twenty.

Your grief has taught you too, Living Dead Dad. Your son was your greatest gift in his life and he is your greatest gift in his death too. Receive it. Let your dead boy be your most profound revelation.

Twenty-one.

Think: *my son's life was twenty-two years long.* Breathe in.

Twenty-two.

Think: *my son's life was twenty-two years long.* Breathe out.

Twenty-three.

There is no twenty-three.

Twenty-four.

Create something of him. Make it beautiful.

Yours,

Sugar

> (*As* **LETTER WRITER #1** *walks away, he reaches a hand back and touches* **SUGAR***'s shoulder. In the moment,* **SUGAR** *feels it.* **LETTER WRITER #1** *takes away his hand.*)
>
> (*For several moments, no one moves onstage.*)

Name Reveal

LETTER WRITER #3. Dear Sugar,

I heard soon you're going to reveal your real name. Is this true? Will we finally know who you are?

Signed,

Hopeful

SUGAR. Dear Hopeful,

There is a common assumption that by not revealing my name, I'm protecting my privacy or it's freeing to write anonymously. But what is freeing is that you can read my responses, without the barriers of whatever preconceptions you might have about my age, my ethnicity, or my achievements. Not knowing my name allows you to have a more pure vision of me.

When I took on Sugar, I wrote the only way I know, and that is with radical sincerity and open arms. What has been the most surprising is how much more you all gave back to me. You gave me,

LETTER WRITER #2 & SUGAR. Love,

LETTER WRITER #2. *(As Sugar's mother.)* Love, love, love, love.

SUGAR. So much love.

Your stories spilled into mine and I spilled mine back into you.

Sugar is not just me. We created something together. We are all Sugar.

I know you and you know me. I've revealed the most intimate details of my life, so keeping my name a secret is no longer important. My name is Cheryl Strayed. Yes, I am Sugar. And so are all of you.

Yours,

Sugar

Tiny Beautiful Things

LETTER WRITER #2. Dear Sugar, I've been wanting to ask you something –

LETTER WRITER #3. My question is pretty simple –

LETTER WRITER #1. It's something I wonder about –

LETTER WRITER #2. What advice would you give your younger self?

LETTER WRITER #3. Love,

You

SUGAR. Dear Younger Me,

Stop worrying about whether you're fat. You're not fat. Actually, you're a little bit fat, but who gives a shit? Feed yourself. The people worthy of your love will love you more for this.

LETTER WRITER #3. The adults who you think are old and stupidly saddled with kids and cars and houses were once every bit as hip and pompous as you.

LETTER WRITER #1. In the middle of the night in the middle of your twenties when a friend crawls naked into your bed, straddles you and says, *You should run away from me before I devour you*...believe her.

LETTER WRITER #2. Don't lament so much about how your career is going to turn out. You don't have a career. You have a life. Keep the faith. Do the work.

The useless days will add up to something. The shitty waitressing jobs. The writing in your journal. The long meandering walks. The hours reading poetry and novels and dead people's diaries and wondering about sex and God and whether you should shave under your arms or not. These things are your becoming.

LETTER WRITER #3. When that sweet but fucked-up gay couple invites you over to their cool house to do ecstasy with them, say no.

LETTER WRITER #2. You cannot convince people to love you. This is an absolute rule. Real love moves freely in both directions. Don't waste your time on anything else.

LETTER WRITER #1. Most things will be okay eventually, but not everything will be. Sometimes you'll put up a good fight and lose. Sometimes you'll hold on hard and realize there is no choice but to let go. Acceptance is a small, quiet room.

LETTER WRITER #3. The night you meet a man in the doorway of a Mexican restaurant who later kisses you while explaining that this kiss doesn't "mean anything" because, much as he likes you, he is not interested in having a relationship right now, just laugh and kiss him back. Your daughter will have his sense of humor. Your son will have his eyes.

LETTER WRITER #1. There are some things you can't understand yet. Your life will be a great and continuous unfolding. You will come to know things that can only be known with the wisdom of age and the grace of years. Most of those things will have to do with forgiveness.

SUGAR. On Christmas at the very beginning of your twenties when your mother gives you a warm coat that she saved for months to buy, don't look at her skeptically after she tells you she thought the coat was perfect for you.

LETTER WRITER #2. Don't hold it up and say it's longer than you like your coats to be and too puffy and possibly even too warm.

LETTER WRITER #1. Your mother will be dead by spring. That coat will be the last gift she gave you.

LETTER WRITER #3. For the rest of your life, you will regret the small thing you didn't say. Say thank you.

> (**SUGAR** *opens the computer and begins to type.*)

SUGAR. During the era in which you've gotten yourself ridiculously tangled up with heroin you will be riding the bus one hot afternoon –

(**SUGAR** *stops typing and addresses the audience.*)

and thinking what a worthless piece of crap you are.

A little girl will get on the bus holding the strings of two purple balloons. She'll offer you one of the balloons, but you won't take it because you believe you no longer have a right to such tiny beautiful things.

You're wrong.

You do.

Yours,
Sugar

(**SUGAR** *turns to* **LETTER WRITER #1**, **LETTER WRITER #2**, *and* **LETTER WRITER #3**, *who then exit.*)

(**SUGAR** *looks at her computer screen one last time, and closes it.* **SUGAR** *stands to go. Then, she picks up a pen and writing journal from the desk. And smiles.*)

(**SUGAR** *goes upstairs.*)

End of Play

CPSIA information can be obtained
at www.ICGtesting.com
Printed in the USA
BVHW060548270221
601178BV00005B/836